Grandfather's Wrinkles

Written by
Kathryn England

Illustrated by
Richard McFarland

Flash
Li ht
PRESS

Lucy climbed onto her grandfather's knee and stared at his smiling face. His skin was like a scrunched-up piece of paper, all crumpled and creased.

"Why doesn't your skin fit you any more, Granddad?" Lucy asked. "It's all crinkly!"

Granddad threw back his head and laughed. "Those crinkles are called wrinkles," he said. "I have lived a very long time and I have wrinkles from smiling so often."

He looked at Lucy's puzzled face and rubbed her cheek. "Whenever I smiled an especially big smile, I got a wrinkle to show for it."

"What's this wrinkle from?" she asked, pointing to a deep crease at the corner of Granddad's right eye.

"Now let me think," he said, scratching his chin. "That's a very old one. Oh yes, I remember. I got that wrinkle from smiling so much the day I married your Grandma."

Lucy pointed to another deep crease at the corner of Granddad's left eye. "What about this one?"

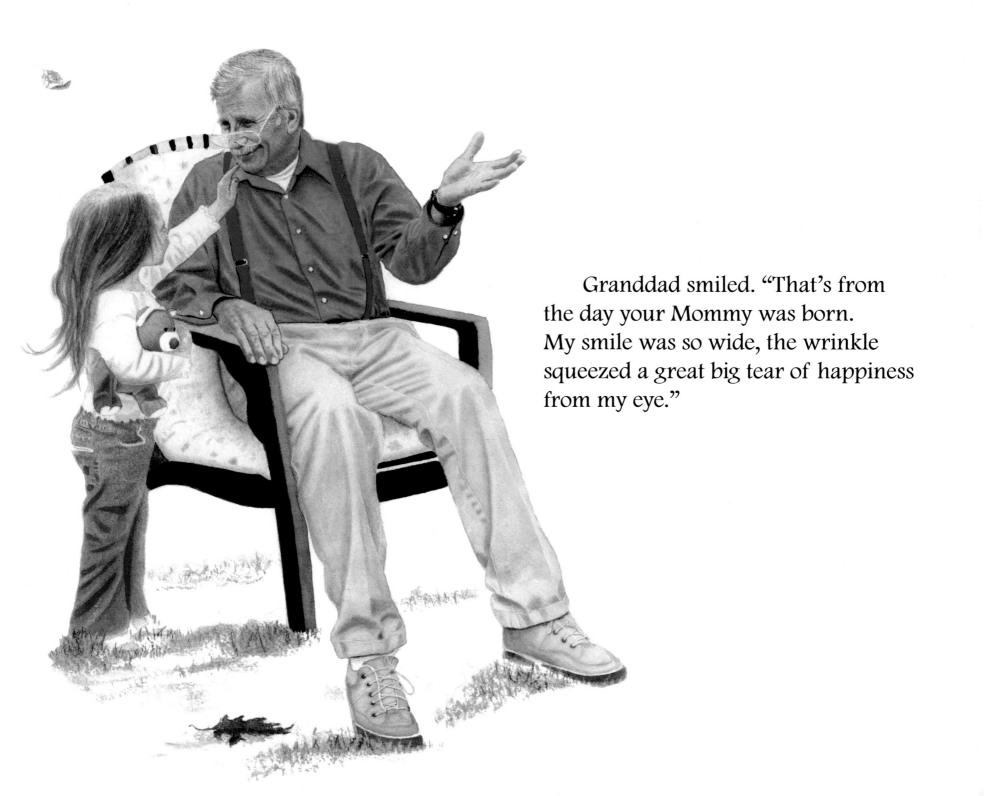

Granddad smiled. "That's from the day your Mommy was born. My smile was so wide, the wrinkle squeezed a great big tear of happiness from my eye."

"And this one here?" Lucy asked, tracing a long wrinkle near her grandfather's nose.

Little grooves appeared between Granddad's thick eyebrows as he thought.

"Now let me see," he said, tapping his head. "Ah, yes. That was the day your Mommy reached into her toy box to get her favorite teddy bear, and fell in!" Granddad laughed.

Lucy giggled. "Mommy must have looked so funny!"

Lucy looked up at Granddad's face again. "Where did this wrinkle come from?" she asked as she ran her chubby finger along a thin line all the way across Granddad's forehead.

"When your Mommy was little," Granddad told Lucy, "Grandma and I took her to a farm. While she was feeding a baby goat, another goat nibbled a piece right out of her shorts. Grandma and I thought it was very funny, but your Mommy didn't."

Lucy smiled as she imagined Mommy's undies showing through the hole in her shorts.

"What are these two from?"
Lucy asked as her fingers traced the
long furrows in her grandfather's
cheeks.

"Oh, those are much more recent
wrinkles," he replied. "I remember
them well. They appeared because
I was so happy the day your Mommy
married your Daddy."

Lucy searched Granddad's face very carefully. "What about these two really, really big ones?" she asked as she put her fingers on the large creases curving up from the corners of Granddad's mouth.

"Ah, those are the most important of all," he told her. "That's why they are the biggest even though they are very new. I got those two extra special wrinkles the day YOU were born."

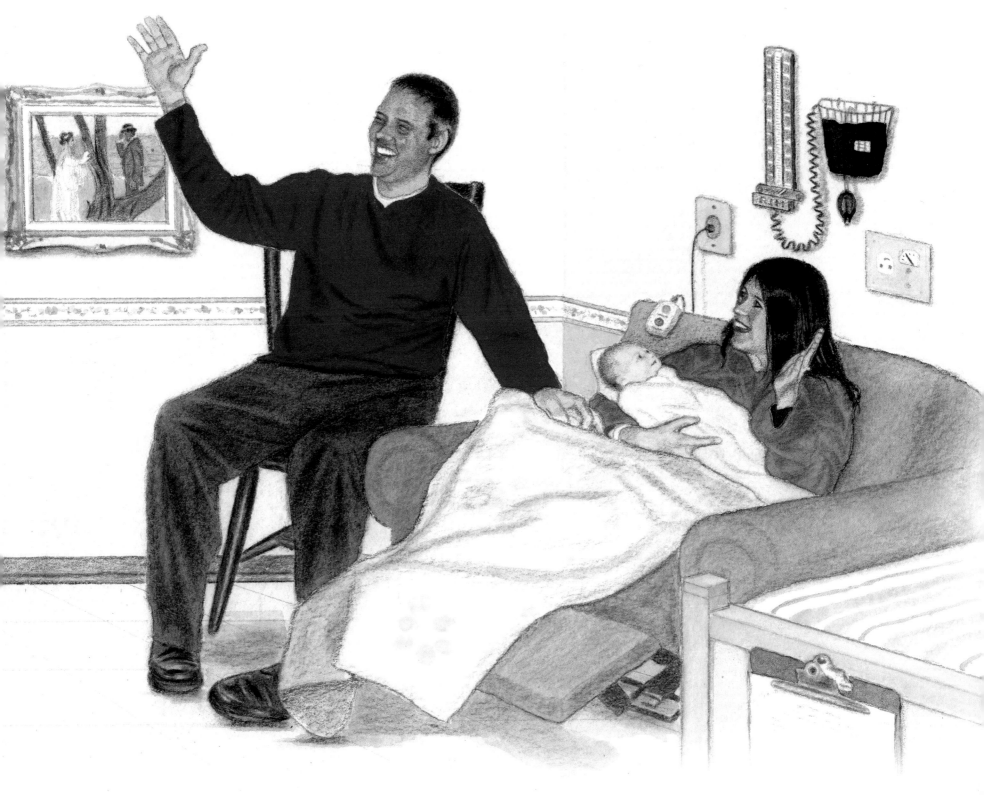

"Oh," said Lucy, smiling a huge smile. And at the corners of her mouth appeared two little wrinkles, just like Granddad's.

For Hayley –KE

To my loving wife Frances, for without her encouragement and compassion,
I'd still be on the drawing board! –RM

Special thanks to Gregg Hangebrauck for recommending this job to me. What a wonderful experience this has been. –RM

Illustration Notes

The following modeled for and appear in this book: Richard McFarland (the illustrator) as Granddad, Bekah Caskey as Lucy, Fran McFarland as Grandma, Thomas and Christine Sherman as Lucy's parents, Rachel Sherman as Lucy's mom as a child, and Annie the cocker spaniel as herself. Also appearing are: Christine, Don and Erma Franks, Gregg Hangebrauck, Frank and Viola Jasonowicz, Chris and Marge Karidis, George King, MaryRose and Mike Krupa, Joe and Mike Lippeth, Christopher McFarland, John D., John Jr. and Lisa Miller, Jeff and Linda Neis, Connie and Ruth Oney, E. George, Eugene, Jake, Mary and Viola Scheuring, Johannah Schultz, Tiffany Scott, Mitch and Pam Szalajka, Emily and Esther Turner, Dina and Dr. Wayne Wagner. The painting that hangs on the wall on page 29 is a scene from the movie *Somewhere in Time*, starring Jane Seymour and Christopher Reeve, for which Richard McFarland painted portraits.